# Been There, Done That

## Reading Animal Signs

*For Jackson~*
*Happy tracking!*
*Jen Funk Weber*

by Jen Funk Weber
illustrated by Andrea Gabriel

"Okay, Helena," said Cole, "where are your wild animals? I go home tomorrow, and all I've seen are magpies and gray jays. Where are the bears and moose?"

"They're out there," said Helena.

Helena and Cole continued on the trail. They wove through willows. The bark was stripped off at waist height. Something had been there. Something had done that. "There are snowshoe hares around here," Helena said.

Cole didn't see any hares.

Months before, when the snow was deep, snowshoe hares nibbled the bark within their reach.

Helena and Cole hiked to a silty, green river.

"Ew!" Cole wrinkled his nose. "Dead fish."

Helena picked up a long, black feather. She traced over wing tips outlined in the sand. Something had been there. Something had done that. "Eagles catch salmon here."

Cole didn't see any eagles.

Earlier that day, an eagle snatched a dying salmon from the water. It hauled the fish up the beach and ate it.

Helena and Cole followed the trail to a sparkling green lake. Helena pointed to cottonwood trunks that looked like apple cores. Something had been there. Something had done that. "Beavers live in that lodge."

Cole didn't see any beavers.

That evening, after the kids left, a beaver crawled out of the lake for a cottonwood snack.

Helena and Cole strolled through a field. Helena sat down in a big oval where the tall grass was smashed flat. Something had been there. Something had done that. "A moose took a nap here."

Cole didn't see any moose.

The day before, a moose waded in the lake, eating sedges from the bottom. Then it lay down in the meadow and snoozed in the sun.

Helena and Cole climbed up a hillside. Helena skipped between little round holes, stopping short at a giant one. Something had been there. Something had done that.

"A bear tried to dig out a ground squirrel."
Cole didn't see any bears.

Early that morning, a grizzly raced after a ground squirrel. The squirrel dove into the nearest hole and zipped through underground tunnels. The grizzly dug and dug, but never found the ground squirrel.

Climbing over the mountain ridge, Helena and Cole discovered a patch of snow on the north side. "So much for all the wild animals," said Cole.

"They're here," Helena assured him. "We just can't see them."

Cole packed snowballs and Helena
made tiny snowmen until a whole herd
of snowmen greeted the setting sun.
"We'd better head home," said Helena.

That night, as the sun crept along the horizon, a red fox trotted over the mountain. It sniffed strange snow statues and tracks.

Something had been there. Something had done that.

# For Creative Minds

This For Creative Minds educational section contains activities to engage children in learning while making it fun at the same time. The activities build on the underlying subjects introduced in the story. While older children may be able to do these activities on their own, we encourage adults to work with the young children in their lives. Even if the adults have long forgotten or never learned this information, they can still work through the activities and be experts in their children's eyes! Exposure to these concepts at a young age helps to build a strong foundation for easier comprehension later in life. This section may be photocopied or printed from our website by the owner of this book for educational, non-commercial uses. Cross-curricular teaching activities for use at home or in the classroom, interactive quizzes, and more are available online. Go to www.ArbordalePublishing.com and click on the book's cover to explore all the links.

## Animal Signs Matching

Match each animal sign or track to the animal that left it. Can you explain how the tracks were made or what the animal was doing when it made them?

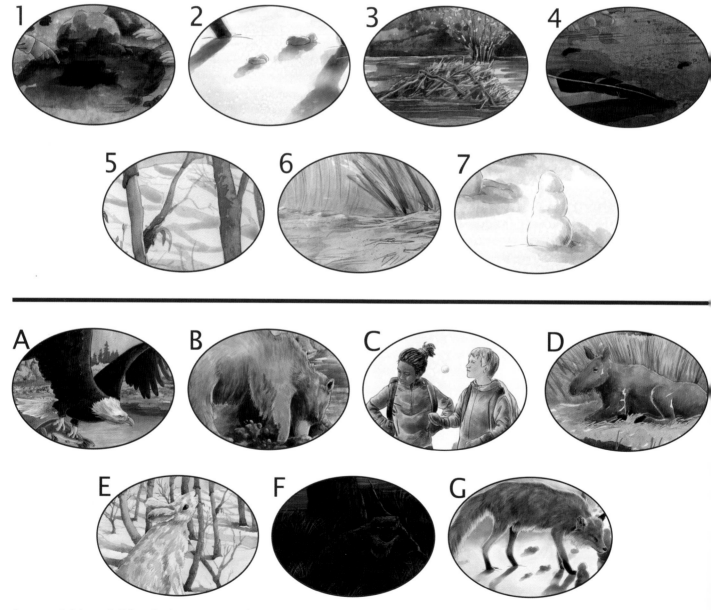

Answers: 1-B bear. 2-G fox. 3-F beaver. 4-A eagle. 5-E hare. 6-D moose. 7-C human.

# Animal Signs Around You

No matter where you are in the world, there are animals around you. What are some animal signs you might see where you live?

All animals leave poop (scat) and urine where they live. Some animals leave other body parts as well. Look for clumps of fur, feathers, or snake skin.
*What body parts can you see?*

All animals need to eat. Look for signs of feeding: stripped logs or branches, chewed leaves and pinecones, bones, or a pile (cache) of nuts and seeds.
*What signs of feeding can you see?*

When animals move, they sometimes leave footprints or other tracks on the ground. Look for tunnels, footprints, slides, or trails through brush.
*What animal tracks can you see?*

Animals need shelter or a place to rest. Look for signs of animal homes: a nest, a beaver lodge, crushed grass, dens in the ground, or holes in banks and trees.
*What signs of shelter can you see?*

## Make a Cast of Tracks

When you look for animal tracks, carry a "cast kit" so you can preserve what you find. Your kit should include: plaster of Paris (or flour and warm water), a plastic bag, old newspaper, and circular strips cut from a two-liter plastic bottle.

Place the plastic circle on the ground so the track is completely inside the circle. In the plastic bag, prepare the plaster of Paris or mix together two cups of flour and one cup warm water. Do not pour directly onto the track—the motion may damage it. Pour your mix onto the ground just inside the edge of the circle. Let it slowly flow into the track and fill it. Wait at least 30-60 minutes.

After your mix has hardened, carefully lift it and wrap it in newspaper to take home. It may still be very fragile. Use a soft brush to clean the dirt away.

You have made a cast of the animal track!

Some animals leave marks behind. Look for markings: grooves in the dirt, muddy wallows, dust baths, or claw or antler marks on trees.
*What markings can you see?*

Animals make all sorts of sounds. Listen for bird calls, frog croaks, insect chirps, bellows, snorts, or barks.
*What animal sounds can you hear?*

# Tracks and Other Signs

## Snowshoe Hare
*Lepus americanus*

Front print: 2-3 inches long, 1.5-2 inches wide
Back print: 4-6 inches long, 2-3.5 inches wide

Hare fur changes color seasonally: brown in the summer, white in the winter. Hares are easiest to spot in the spring and fall when their coats don't match their surroundings.

When hares hop fast, their big back feet sometimes land in front of their front feet, which makes for some confusing tracks.

Snowshoe hares "scream" when in danger and thump their hind feet to send warnings.

## Bald Eagle
*Haliaeetus leucocephalus*

Wing span: 6-8 feet

Young bald eagles are mottled brown. They develop white head- and tailfeathers when they mature at 4 or 5 years of age. Look for white spots on top of dead trees and near the trunks of live ones to spot an eagle.

Eagles return to the same nests year after year, making repairs and additions over time. Some eagle nests are 10 feet across (ten feet is like two sixth graders standing one on top of the other.) Look for nests in leafy or dead trees—not spruce trees—near lakes, rivers, and other wetlands.

Eagles mostly eat fish and dead animals (carrion). You might see wing marks and tracks in sand or snow.

## Beaver
*Castor canadensis*

Front print: 2.5-4 inches long, 2-3.5 inches wide
Back print: 5-7 inches long, 3.3-5.3 inches wide

Beavers build dams across streams to create ponds where they can live, safe from predators. They build lodges in ponds, or dig dens along the banks of rivers.

Beavers eat bark from trees, then use the stripped logs for building. Look for gnawed trees and stumps, lodges, and dams.

In the fall, beavers cut and store branches for winter food. They secure the branches in mud at the bottom of their ponds. Look for a cache of branches near beaver lodges.

## Moose
### Alces alces

Prints: 4-7 inches long (11 inches with dewclaws), 3.5-6 inches wide

Moose can weigh up to 1,800 pounds. When one lies down, it can make a big dent in the snow or grass.

Moose eat willows, birch, and other plants. Look for nipped-off branches.

Moose hair catches on branches. The long, squiggly, gray and white hairs often have dark tips and are hollow. Hollow hair traps air to keep the moose warm.

Male moose lose their antlers every winter, then start growing new ones in the spring.

## Grizzly bear
### Ursus arctos

Front print: 5-7 inches long, 4-6 inches wide
Back print: 9-12 inches long, 5-7 inches wide

Tracks and scat are the most common bear signs. Bears' front feet and back feet make different tracks. You might fit your whole shoe inside a large grizzly bear track.

Bears rub their backs and scratch their claws on trees, leaving clumps of hair and claw marks. Hair can vary in color from light tan to dark brown. Look for these scratches on trees.

Bears sometimes bury prey they've killed, storing it for a later meal.

If you see any signs of bears, be alert! Bears can be dangerous.

## Human
### Homo sapiens

Hand prints: 6.7-7.5 inches long, 3-3.5 inches wide
Foot prints: 9.2-10.3 inches long, 3.5-4 inches wide

Human beings live all around the world, in all kinds of habitats. They have a variety of skin, hair, and eye colors.

Humans are the only mammal in the world to walk on two feet for most of their lives. They live in communities, family groups, and alone. They make countless noises. Humans build houses and roads, drive cars, ride bikes, walk, canoe, and swim.

Look around. There are signs of humans everywhere!

To those who make tracks but are rarely seen, and to those who notice and appreciate them.—JFW

With special thanks to Lulu Hestad and Mason Pittman for their enthusiastic help with the artwork in this book.—AG

The author donates a portion of her royalties to First Book (www.firstbook.org).

Thanks to Ute Olsson, Chief Naturalist at the Eagle River Nature Center, for reviewing the accuracy of the information in this book.

Library of Congress Cataloging-in-Publication Data

Names: Weber, Jen Funk, author. | Gabriel, Andrea, illustrator.
Title: Been there, done that : reading animal signs / by Jen Funk Weber ;
   illustrated by Andrea Gabriel.
Description: Mount Pleasant, SC : Arbordale Publishing, 2016. | Summary: When
   Cole's visit with his friend Helena nears its end, he asks where all the
   wild animals are and she takes him on a trail, showing signs of beavers,
   snowshoe hares, eagles, and more along the way. Includes activities. |
   Includes bibliographical references.
Identifiers: LCCN 2015030416| ISBN 9781628557275 (english hardcover) | ISBN
   9781628557343 (english pbk.) | ISBN 9781628557480 (english downloadable
   ebook) | ISBN 9781628557626 (english interactive dual-language ebook) |
   ISBN 9781628557411 (spanish pbk.) | ISBN 9781628557558 (spanish
   downloadable ebook) | ISBN 9781628557695 (spanish interactive
   dual-language ebook)
Subjects: | CYAC: Tracking and trailing--Fiction. | Animal tracks--Fiction. |
   Nature study--Fiction.
Classification: LCC PZ7.1.W423 Bee 2016 | DDC [E]--dc23 LC record
available at http://lccn.loc.gov/2015030416

Available in Spanish: *Alguien ha estado aquí, alguien lo ha hecho:
descifrando las señales de los animales*.
Lexile® Level: AD 500
key phrases: Environmental Education, Animal Signs/Tracks

Bibliography:
Alaska Department of Fish and Game. Alaska Wildlife
   Notebook Series. Updated in 2008.
Ewing, Susan. The Great Alaska Nature Factbook.
   Alaska Northwest Books, Seattle, WA 1996.
Reardon, Jim. Alaska Mammals. Alaska Geographic, Vol. 8,
   No. 2, 1981.
Sheldon, Ian and Hartson, Tamara. Animal Tracks of Alaska.
   Lone Pine Field Guide. Lone Pine Publishing, Auburn, WA, 1999.

Manufactured in China, December 2015
This product conforms to CPSIA 2008
First Printing

Arbordale Publishing
Mt. Pleasant, SC 29464
www.ArbordalePublishing.com